Ron Rabbit is collecting things.

Ron collects a tin,

a tap,

a pot and

a lid.

Ron collects a plug,

a plank and

a pump.

Next, Ron collects a spring,

a strap and

lots of string.

Clink clink!

Bang bang!

Prod prod!

Crank crank!

Twist twist!

It's a rocket!

Lift-off!

But then...

Splash!

It's not a rocket.

It's a submarine!